3 1994 00907 9267

SANTA ANA PUBLIC LIBRARY

D0536033

SANTA ANA PUBLIC LIBRARY

DICK KING-SMITH
THE SPOTTY PIG

Pictures by
MARY WORMELL

Farrar, Straus and Giroux
New York

J PICT BK KING-SMITH,
King-Smith, Dick.
The spotty pig /
                1400
      31994009079267

BKM
BOOKMOBILE 1 31994009079267

Text copyright © 1997 by Foxbusters Ltd.
Pictures copyright © 1997 by Mary Wormell
All rights reserved
Library of Congress catalog card number: 96–61437
First published in Great Britain by Victor Gollancz Ltd. 1997
Printed and bound in Hong Kong by Imago Publishing Ltd.
First American edition, 1997

"How ugly spots are!" said Peter, the spotty piglet,
to his friend, a cat called Joe.

All through the summer, Peter lay in the sun.
If my spots fade, he thought,
no one will notice them.

At the end of the summer, he asked Joe,
"Can you still see my spots?"
"Sure," said Joe. "You've grown a little bigger,
  so they've grown a little bigger, too."
"Oh, brush my bristles!" cried Peter.

All through the autumn, Peter rolled in the fallen leaves. If I'm really dirty, he thought, no one will notice my spots.

At the end of the autumn, he asked Joe,
"Can you still see my spots?"
"You betcha," said Joe.
"You've grown quite a lot bigger,
  so they've grown quite a lot bigger, too."
"Oh, twirl my tail!" cried Peter.

All through the winter, Peter played in the snow.
Perhaps I can freeze my spots, he thought,
and then they'll all turn white
and no one will notice them.

At the end of the winter, he asked Joe,
"Have my spots gone?"
"You must be joking," said Joe.
"You've grown much bigger, so your
   spots have grown much bigger, too."
"Oh, shiver my shanks!" cried Peter.

All through the spring, Peter stood in the rain.
Perhaps I can wash off my spots, he thought,
and then no one will ever see them again.

At the end of the spring, he asked Joe,
"Now have my spots gone?"
"Listen, sonny," said the cat. "You are now
a very large pig, and you are covered in very large spots."
"Oh no," shouted Peter. "Snuffle my snout and
tweak my trotters! I SHALL NEVER
GET RID OF MY SPOTS!"

"I hope you don't," came a voice behind him.
"They suit you."
Peter spun around to see
a beautiful young pig. She, too,
was covered with spots. Oh, thought Peter,
perhaps spots aren't so bad, after all.

"My name," said the young pig, "is Penny.
How do you do?"

"Oh, very well, thank you!" said Peter joyfully.
"You've taken a weight off his mind," purred Joe.

From then on, Peter and Penny spent their days

together, doing all the things that pigs do.

They rootled in the ground together and wallowed in the

mud together, and Peter never gave a thought to spots.

Until the day that Penny gave birth to thirteen piglets.

"Well, bless my piggy eyes!" called Peter to his friend Joe.
"Just look at these babies!"

"Spotted something about them, have you?" said Joe.
"Yes," said Peter. "How beautiful spots are!"